The Littles
and the Big Blizzard

The Littles and the Big Blizzard

Adapted by **Teddy Slater**
from **THE LITTLES TO THE RESCUE**
by **John Peterson**
Illustrated by **Jacqueline Rogers**

SCHOLASTIC INC.
New York Toronto London Auckland Sydney
Mexico City New Delhi Hong Kong

William T. Little was very small.

In fact, he was only six inches tall.

But he had a very big family,

and Mr. Little's family was

about to get even bigger.

His wife was expecting

a baby any time now.

Tom and Lucy Little could not
wait to meet their new
brother or sister.
Granny Little and Uncle Pete
were just as excited.
They all lived together
inside the walls of the Biggs' house.

6

"I hope Aunt Lily gets here soon,"

Mrs. Little said.

"I can't have this baby without her."

Aunt Lily was a nurse.

Her son Dinky was a pilot.

He was going to fly her from

their house to the Biggs' house

in his glider.

But this was no night

for flying.

A big blizzard was blowing.

"Check your parachute, Mother,"

Dinky yelled into the wind.

"We're in for a rough ride."

"I'm all set," Aunt Lily said.

"Let's go!"

The howling winds tossed
the glider up and down
and around and around.

Dinky could hardly see

where he was going.

But finally Dinky spotted
the bright light on the Biggs' porch.
He carefully guided the
tiny plane onto the roof.

Dinky jumped out of the glider.

"We made it!" he cried.

But when he turned to help

his mother out of her seat...

...the seat was empty!

"Oh, no!" Dinky cried.

"Mother must have fallen out!"

Dinky took off again.

All night long he searched

for his mother.

But all he could see

was the swirling snow.

15

As the new day dawned,

Dinky finally gave up

and flew back

to the Biggs' house.

"My poor mother is lost in the storm," he told the other Littles.

"You men must find her!"

Mrs. Little said.

"It's hopeless," Dinky sighed.

"I looked everywhere."

"But you were way up in the air,"

Mr. Little pointed out.

"We can look from the ground."

"It might take us days to

walk that far," Dinky said.

"No problem," said Tom.

"We can get Hildy to carry us!"

Hildy was the Biggs' cat
and a fine friend of Tom's.
She was the only Bigg who
even knew the Littles existed.
Tom asked Hildy to help them.
She seemed to understand.

The three Little men and Tom
climbed onto Hildy's back,
and they headed for the cold outdoors.

The snow had stopped falling.

The whole world was

sparkly white.

Tom steered the big cat

by gently tugging on her ears.

22

Hildy picked her way through the
cold snow.

"What's that?" Uncle Pete called out.

Something was moving under the bush.

It was only a rabbit.

Hildy walked on.

The Littles kept their eyes

open for any sign of

the tiny nurse.

"Look, there!" Tom shouted.

"It's Mother's parachute!"
Dinky called out.

"And I can see her footprints
in the snow," Tom said.

"Let's follow them."

Aunt Lily's tracks went

this way and that way

and that way and this way.

They finally ended...

right at the Biggs' house!

Tom and the men jumped off Hildy

and ran to the secret door

that led to the Littles' apartment.

Mr. Little could hear
strange sounds in the bedroom.
Slowly he opened the door.

There was Aunt Lily!

Mrs. Little was sitting up in bed

with a soft, pink bundle

in her arms.

Granny and Lucy were

sitting next to her.

"Aunt Lily!" Tom cried.

"We've been looking all over

for you."

Aunt Lily put a finger to her lips.

"Hush," she said.

"You'll wake up your sister."

"Come here, Tom,
and look at baby Betsy,"
said Lucy.

"She is so *tiny*!"